The Boxcar Children Mysteries
by Gertrude Chandler Warner

THE BOXCAR CHILDREN
SURPRISE ISLAND
THE YELLOW HOUSE MYSTERY
MYSTERY RANCH
MIKE'S MYSTERY
BLUE BAY MYSTERY
THE WOODSHED MYSTERY
THE LIGHTHOUSE MYSTERY
MOUNTAIN TOP MYSTERY
SCHOOLHOUSE MYSTERY
CABOOSE MYSTERY
HOUSEBOAT MYSTERY
SNOWBOUND MYSTERY
TREE HOUSE MYSTERY
BICYCLE MYSTERY
MYSTERY IN THE SAND
MYSTERY BEHIND THE WALL
BUS STATION MYSTERY
BENNY UNCOVERS A MYSTERY
THE HAUNTED CABIN MYSTERY
THE DESERTED LIBRARY MYSTERY

HE DESERTED LIBRARY MYSTERY

created by
GERTRUDE CHANDLER WARNER

Illustrated by Charles Tang

ALBERT WHITMAN & Company
Morton Grove, Illinois

ISBN 0-8075-1560-4

Copyright © 1991 by Albert Whitman & Company. All rights reserved. Published simultaneously in Canada by General Publishing, Limited, Toronto. THE BOXCAR CHILDREN is a registered trademark of Albert Whitman & Company.

7 9 11 13 12 10 8   4 5 6 7/9

Printed in the U.S.A.

40

Contents

CHAPTER 1

Grandfather's News

Grandfather Alden sat in a lawn chair and poured a glass of lemonade. It was a hot August day with the sky a bright blue. When Violet went by, he said, "Violet, dear, call the others, will you?"

"Yes, Grandfather," she answered. Ten-year-old Violet was a lovely girl who was shy and sweet.

In a few minutes all four of the grandchildren sat on the grass before Mr. Alden. Henry, Jessie, Violet, and Benny loved their grandfather. They remembered when their parents had died and they had run away to hide in a boxcar. They had heard their grandfather was a mean old man, and they had been afraid that he would find them. When Violet became ill and a doctor was needed, the doctor told her grandfather about the children. It was then they went to live with him, and discovered that Grandfather wasn't mean at all. He was kind and good. He always encouraged them to follow their own ideas.

Grandfather Alden poured each child a glass of cold lemonade, then leaned back in his chair. "I have some interesting news for you," he said, his warm smile widening.

Henry and Jessie leaned forward. What could his news be? Violet was quiet as usual, but her eyes were big with curiosity. Benny, the youngest, only six, couldn't stand it any longer. He jumped up and danced around his grandfather. "What is it?" he asked.

Grandfather laughed. He knew how much Benny loved an adventure. In fact, they all loved an adventure. Even Watch, their dog, who lay at Jessie's feet.

Grandfather became serious. "I've just talked to Pete Hanson."

"Doesn't he own the café and bait shop in Rock Falls near the bay?" Henry asked.

"Yes, he does," Grandfather answered. "Pete told me that the small village's old library is going to be torn down. You know it hasn't been used in many years."

"Why?" Benny asked.

"Well," Grandfather said, "not only were there not enough people in town, but when the librarian left several years ago, no one took her place."

"I remember seeing the boarded-up library once," twelve-year-old Jessie said.

"I don't remember!" Benny shouted. "I want to see it!"

"I think we're all about to see the library, Benny," Henry said. He looked at his grandfather. "Isn't that right?"

"That's right, Henry," Grandfather Alden replied. Henry was only fourteen, but he was wise and understanding. Grandfather finished his lemonade and said, "That library belongs to the town of Rock Falls, and it has shelves and shelves of old books that probably need to be sorted out. I remember that lovely library building when I was young. My family had a house in Rock Falls where we spent our summers."

"How young were you?" Benny asked.

"I was a little boy like you," Grandfather said. "And I was fond of the old library, and now I want to see the town council give it landmark status."

"What is landmark status, Grandfather?" This time Violet asked the question.

"When a building is saved by the public so that everyone can enjoy its history. Wouldn't you like to explore the place and see what's in the library? And neaten it up so it looks good enough to be a landmark?"

"Yes, yes!" Benny said. "An adventure! When can we go?"

"You can leave tomorrow," Grandfather said, a twinkle in his eyes. "I've received permission from Pete. You see, Pete owns a small house on the edge of the village. During the summer months he lives and works in his restaurant and in the winter he lives in his house, carving and painting fish lures."

Jessie stood up. Even though she was two years younger than Henry, she always knew what needed to be done. "How wonderful to be able to stay in Pete's house. We'll need bedding, food, and some cooking pots."

"No cooking pots or bedding." Grandfather laughed. "You'll find Pete's place is well equipped. You'll even find some canned and packaged goods on the shelf. All you'll need to bring is fresh food. Later, you can go to Pete's Café and buy what you need." He handed a key to Henry. "This will unlock Pete's house." Next he handed a key to Jessie. "And this is for the library. Pete sent both to me."

"Thanks, Grandfather," Jessie said.

Grandfather reached down and scratched Watch's ear. "You stay with me, Watch. Otherwise, I'll be lonesome."

"Let's start packing," Henry said. His dark blue eyes were sparkling with excitement.

They all ran into their house except Violet. She stooped down and kissed Grandfather's forehead. "Thank you," she said softly.

"You're welcome, Violet." Grandfather's eyes softened. How lucky he was to have such loving grandchildren.

The next morning the Alden children set off on their bicycles. Their backpacks and baskets contained supplies and clothing. They pedaled for two hours. Henry was ahead. Jessie and Violet followed, and Benny was behind. Even though Benny pedaled as fast as his legs would go, he was last. "Wait for me," he yelled. "I'm hungry!" He stopped in the middle of the road.

Jessie laughed. "You're always hungry, Benny." But she slowed down and stopped.

"I know," Benny said, smiling.

"Look," Violet said, pointing to two large oak trees with a small stream beside them. "Wouldn't that be a perfect scene to paint?"

"That's a perfect place for a picnic," Henry said. He jumped off his bike and wheeled it off the road.

Benny parked his red bike by the roadside, too.

Jessie spread a checked tablecloth on the

soft green grass. Violet poured milk into paper cups and they all drank from them, except Benny, of course. He had his pink cracked cup. He'd found it in a dump when they lived in the boxcar, and wouldn't part with it. Henry reached for the thermos and refilled the cups. Benny quickly took out four ham sandwiches from the picnic basket, and they began to eat.

An orange-and-black butterfly hovered over their food.

"That's a big butterfly!" Benny shouted. "It might eat my sandwich."

Henry chuckled. "No, it won't. You've already eaten most of it. The poor monarch butterfly won't even get a crumb."

After they'd eaten sweet purple grapes for dessert, they once again got on their bikes.

"Only a few more miles," Henry said. He studied his compass. "The library is straight east of here."

Jessie started to sing:

"Row, row, row your boat
Gently down the stream."

Soon everyone joined in.

After riding a couple of miles, and going through the tiny town of Rock Falls, Henry said, pointing, "There it is. Pete gave Grandfather perfect directions." Pete's house, surrounded by trees and bushes, looked neat and well kept. Off in the distance stood the library, a gray shingled building with windows boarded up and the roof sagging in the middle. Even farther away sparkled a green sea.

They pedaled faster.

When they reached Pete's house, they saw it had an upstairs window that looked out toward the water. They stopped.

"Oooh," Benny whispered. "The house looks so lonely. Maybe ghosts live there when Pete is gone for the summer."

"Nonsense," Henry replied. "Let's go inside." He sounded cheerful, but secretly he agreed with Benny. There was something scary about this place. Henry glanced about. No one was in sight. He looked over his shoulder. He was sure something would happen here. Their visit might not be as much fun as everyone thought.

CHAPTER 2

The Old Library

Henry unlocked the deserted house and went in first. The sun streamed through the window.

He motioned the others to follow. Slowly they went in. The wooden floor creaked. The first large room had a table with five chairs. A stool sat in the corner by a stone fireplace, and a wood-burning stove was in the center of the room. A huge cobweb stretched across one corner.

"Look!" Jessie exclaimed. "A stove! We can have a fine hot supper."

Benny smiled. "That's good news. But it's broken."

"It will be easy to fix," Violet said. "Only the oven door is off its hinges."

"Don't worry," said Jessie. "I can push it back in place." She opened and closed the squeaking cast-iron door.

Next they went into a bedroom. Two bunk beds were against one wall. A sagging string held up a tattered curtain at the window. It was clear Pete had other things on his mind besides keeping house.

"Neat!" Benny shouted. He dashed to the beds' ladder and climbed up to the top bunk. He bounced up and down on the mattress, causing the dust to fly. "I want this bed!" he yelled.

"You're welcome to it," Henry said, sitting on the bottom bunk. He coughed. "Whew! Too much dust!" He glanced at Jessie. "Where shall we begin?"

Jessie nodded. She knew exactly what to do. She'd already run upstairs and found two more bunk beds up there. "First, we need to clean the two windows in this room and the two in the kitchen. That way we can see outside."

"Why?" Henry asked, rubbing off the window grime so that he had a small peephole. "There's nothing to see. No one is in this desolate area but us, and there isn't even a phone in the house."

Violet swallowed. "No one but us?" she asked in a low voice. "That gives me the creeps."

"We're safe as we can be," Henry said. "Pete's restaurant is only two miles away."

"I know," Violet said, but she didn't sound reassured.

"Next," Jessie said matter-of-factly to show she wasn't nervous and to help Violet, "we'll take the four mattresses outside and whale the daylights out of them."

"Right!" Henry grinned. "Unless Benny wants to bounce the dust out!"

"No, no," Violet said.

"Just teasing," Henry said. He rolled up his sleeves and lifted a mattress over his shoulder and headed for the door. "Come on, Benny," he called. "We'll do one at a time."

Eagerly Benny scrambled down the ladder.

"Violet," Jessie said, "let's tackle the floor. I saw an old broom and a mop by the stove. There was a pail, too."

"Right," Violet agreed. "This floor could use a scrubbing."

"It could use two scrubbings," Jessie said, tying a scarf over her hair. "Let's get started."

"Where's the water?" Violet questioned.

Jessie pointed out the window. "See that pump? We'll have plenty of fresh water, and there's a dry sink in the house."

Jessie fetched a pail of water, bubbling with soap suds because of the detergent she'd added.

First the girls scrubbed the kitchen, then the bedrooms. The floors began to shine.

The boys went in and out with first one mattress, then another. The four Aldens worked all afternoon. They washed the windows and cleaned the stove.

Benny came in and wiped his forehead, smudging a streak of dirt even further across his face. He dropped into a chair. "Whew!

We pounded four mattresses. We washed four windows. I'm tired and . . ."

"I know," Violet said with a laugh. "You're tired *and* hungry."

Benny cocked his head to one side. "How did you know what I was going to say?"

"We all know what you were about to say," Henry said. Playfully he poked Benny in the ribs. "Besides, I'm hungry, too."

"So am I," Violet said.

"Me, too," Jessie agreed.

Henry threw back his head and laughed. "Then it's a majority. Let's unload the supplies and eat."

Jessie went out to the pump to wash her face and hands.

Next Violet went out to the pump, then Henry, then Benny.

"We'll need wood for the stove," Jessie said.

"I'm way ahead of you," Henry replied with a smile. "There's a bundle of wood by the front door."

Jessie peeled potatoes and onions and scraped the carrots. Henry set a pot of water on the stove. When the water boiled, the girls dropped in a soup bone they had brought and the vegetables.

"A hot supper will taste good," Jessie said.

"I'll say it will." Benny rolled his eyes and patted his stomach. It didn't take too long for the soup to cook. With a crusty bread they had brought from home and fresh pears and cookies, they had a delicious meal.

After supper Violet sat on the window ledge. "There's the library," she said softly.

"Where?" Benny asked eagerly, craning his neck to see.

"On the hill over there." Violet gazed at the gray building. "How sad and lonely it looks."

"We'll cheer the old place up tomorrow," Jessie said. "We'll be chattering and going through its old books."

"Oh, yes," Benny said, clapping his hands. "We'll make the library happy. We're going to save it."

But that night before Violet got into bed, she stared out the window. She wondered if anything could save the old library.

CHAPTER 3

The Squirrel That Wasn't There

The next morning, before anyone awakened, Henry quietly went outside and mounted his bicycle. He pedaled down the winding path and rode the two miles to Pete's Café. He must phone Grandfather and tell him they'd arrived safely.

The air smelled salty, and the sunny day warmed him. He felt good. They were off on another adventure.

Entering the café, Henry smiled at a plump man with a white beard behind the counter. He knew he must be Pete. "Hi, I'm

Henry Alden. James Alden is my grandfather. My sisters and brother and I are living in your house for a few days," Henry said.

"Hi, Henry," the plump man said. "Good to meet you. How do you like my house?"

"Fine," Henry answered. He didn't want to tell him how much cleaning they'd had to do.

Pete chuckled. "I imagine the cobwebs and dust were pretty thick after my house had been sitting there for all these months. I guess you and your sisters and brother took care of things."

"We did a little cleaning," Henry said with a smile.

"Did you find the extra pillows in the closet by the back door?"

"Yes, we've found everything we need," Henry assured him.

"And the pump worked okay?"

"Yes, and so did the stove and refrigerator," Henry said. "I need to use the phone to tell Grandfather we're all right."

"Go right ahead," Pete said. "And tell him hello for me."

As Henry dialed, he overheard two men who were sitting at a nearby table.

The first man leaned forward. "Did you hear Mrs. Tate was robbed of her diamond ring last week?"

"You're kidding!" the second man said in surprise. "That's the third robbery in two months. Some antique maps were taken from Tom Davis's map and coin shop, and Mike Johnson's jewelry store was robbed, too. Who do you suppose is doing it?"

"Beats me," the first man said. "But we'd all better keep things under lock and key."

Henry promised himself that *they'd* better be careful and lock Pete's door.

After talking to Grandfather, Henry said good-bye to Pete and biked back to the house.

He arrived just in time for breakfast, and then they all biked to the library, which was about a quarter of a mile away. Because the narrow winding lane was steep, Benny had to stop several times.

When they reached the library, they stopped to stare at the gray shingled build-

ing. It tilted to one side, and the ground floor windows were boarded up. The front concrete steps were chipped and broken, and the roof had lost half its shingles.

The second floor had a large window looking to the sea. Because no one had boarded it up, a few glass panes were missing. It was as if the library had one big eye watching the water. Watching and waiting. What was it that Violet had said? Jessie thought. The library looked sad and lonely.

"Wow!" Benny uttered, a light breeze rumpling his dark shiny hair. "It's scary!"

Jessie pushed her strange thoughts away. "Let's see for ourselves," she said brightly. She moved to the first step.

"Okay," Benny said. "I'm right behind you."

Henry laughed, taking Violet's hand. "This is going to be fun."

Jessie unlocked the door.

After they entered the dark and silent library, they halted. Surprise was written on their faces. Shelves of books lined the room, but many more books were scattered on the floor, some face down. Others were thrown in a corner. In the center of the room was a large desk that had been the circulation desk.

They walked further into the room. Henry bravely went upstairs. "Come on," he urged. His brother and sisters followed. They went into a room that also had books, but there was a large reading area by the big window. Under the window was a long seat covered in faded and worn material.

"This velvet seat was once red," Jessie said, brushing her fingertips over the cushion.

"It looks pink to me!" Benny said. His voice echoed through the whole room.

"All right," Henry said, "before we go through the books, I'll remove the boards from the downstairs windows." He was dressed for work, too, in his jeans, and a shirt with a red stripe and short sleeves. "If we make the library look good, it may be given the landmark status Grandfather wants so much."

"It would be wonderful to be able to do that for him," Violet said.

"I'll help you, Henry," Benny said, running downstairs.

"Careful," Jessie cautioned. "Some of those wooden steps might be broken."

"I'm okay," Benny said. "See?" He stood at the bottom of the steps, looking up. His hands were behind his back, and he wore a big grin.

"Good, Benny," Henry said. "Here we come." They hurried down after Benny.

They all pitched in. The boards were removed from the windows, letting the sunlight stream in. They dusted and cleaned until Benny said, "Isn't it time for lunch yet?"

Violet halted, wiping her forehead. "Yes, I'm ready for a sandwich, too." She sat down, straightening the collar on her violet T-shirt. Violet was her favorite color. She even had wallpaper in her room at home with violets on it.

"Lunch will be later," Jessie said. "It's only eleven o'clock."

Willingly, they straightened more books.

"Look," Benny said, holding up a volume

of fairy tales. It was an old book with no cover, but the pages were still in good condition. "Read me this story, Jessie," he said, pointing to one.

Jessie, who was on her knees, stood up and took a deep breath. "I'm ready for a break. We'll sit over here by the circulation desk, Benny. Ah, you've chosen *Rumpelstiltskin*." She began to read about the maiden who was forced to weave all day, and the threads she wove that turned to gold.

When Jessie finished the story, Benny stood up. "Wow!" he exclaimed, "Rumpelstiltskin was a mean man. I'd like to spin gold!"

"And what would you do with it, Benny?" Jessie asked, a twinkle in her eyes.

"I'd fix up this old library for Grandfather," he said promptly.

"That's a great idea," Henry said, joining them. "Right now, though, rest time is over."

"Is it lunchtime?" Benny asked.

"Not yet," Henry chuckled, lightly touching Benny's chin with his fist. "We've got hundreds of books to straighten."

"Okay," Benny said cheerfully. "But I'm going upstairs."

"Will you place the books neatly on the shelves?" Violet asked.

"I sure will!"

And before anyone could say another word, Benny raced upstairs.

Jessie smiled. "I hope he's this eager to help by late afternoon."

"Look at this old speller I found," Violet said, handing a thin book to Jessie.

Jessie wrinkled her small nose. "It smells musty." She handed the book back. "We'd better finish these shelves." She pulled out a book and flipped through its pages. All at once she gasped. "A moth! It flew right in my face."

Violet glimpsed a winged insect flying out the window. "What next?" she asked, with a sigh.

Suddenly Benny rushed downstairs. His round face was pale, and his lower lip trembled.

"Benny! What happened?" Jessie asked in

a concerned tone. "You're as white as a sheet."

"I-I heard a noise," he said in a quavering voice. "Someone is up there."

Jessie glanced at Violet and Henry, then turned back to Benny. "Just what did you hear, Benny?"

"It was kind of a little sound, and then I saw a big black shadow!"

"We'll all go upstairs and look around," Violet said. She put her arm around Benny's shoulders. "Maybe it was a squirrel hiding a nut."

Benny shook his head. "No. Someone was there! I know it!"

They went upstairs and searched every row of books and every corner. "No one's here, Benny," Jessie said, tousling her brother's hair. "Maybe the squirrel went out through the broken windowpane."

"M-maybe," he stammered. But Benny glanced at the stairs. Not for a minute did he believe it was a squirrel. Violet, too, had a nervous look on her face.

CHAPTER 4

The Missing Food

"It's almost time for lunch, Benny," Henry announced. He wanted to take Benny's mind off the strange noise. Food usually did the trick.

"Is it time to eat?" Benny looked at Henry. "I forgot."

"You forgot lunch?" Jessie teased. "That's hard to believe."

Benny was wiping one last shelf. But all at once his rag snagged on a dark object in back. "What's this?" he said, holding up a strange piece of metal. "Look, everybody!"

They gathered around Benny, and Henry carefully examined what he had found.

"This is the hilt of a sword," Jessie said. "Whew! It must be covered with six coats of grime! But where's the rest of it?" she wondered.

Violet reached for a crumpled piece of yellow paper that dangled from the hilt by a worn ribbon. Carefully she unfolded the square sheet and began to read:

> This sword is presented to Captain Charles Howard for his bravery at the Battle of Gettysburg. Your strength and courage in leading the Union soldiers against General Robert E. Lee's forces was a major factor in winning this vital battle.
>
> Signed,
>
> General G.G. Meade
> Union Commander
> July 5, 1863

The children gasped.

Henry sat down in a chair and turned the hilt every which way.

"What's Gettysburg?" Benny asked.

Henry leaned back. "Gettysburg, Pennsylvania, was where one of the most important battles of the Civil War was fought."

"Wasn't General Lee the Confederate leader who led his army on an attack against the North?" Violet asked.

"That's right," Jessie said. "If he had won, the whole outcome of the war might have been different. Our country would have been split in two. Today the North would have their own flag, and the South would have theirs."

"Wow," Benny whispered. "Then this is valuable, isn't it?"

"Yes, it is," Henry said. "It would be even more valuable if we could find the blade."

Jessie took the sword hilt and wrapped it in a towel. "We'll keep the hilt under the desk. I'm certain we'll find the rest of the sword." She smiled. "In the meantime, we'll have lunch. We'll fix our own sandwiches. I brought a jar of strawberry jam and a jar of peanut butter."

"And I brought the bread," Violet said.

"And I brought the milk," Henry added.

"And I brought the appetite!" Benny yelled. He glanced around. "Good-bye, squirrel, and don't come back!"

After they had eaten, Jessie looked into her backpack. "You know what? We still each have an apple to eat."

Benny said, "Not for me. I ate two sandwiches."

"Then I'll leave them here for our snack tomorrow." Jessie put the sack on top of the circulation desk.

They continued to work until late afternoon. Then Henry said, "Enough. We'll finish tomorrow."

They were all tired and dirty and glad to return to their cozy house. The bunk beds were made, the stove shone, and the old pump in the back gave them fresh water to wash in.

* * *

After dinner and a good night's sleep, the children awoke refreshed and hurried back to the library. Jessie put their lunch basket on the desk next to the apples. She checked the sack and was astonished to see only three apples. "That's funny!" she said. "I *know* there were four apples here yesterday."

Benny laughed. "Jessie made a mistake," he sang out.

Jessie laughed, too. But she was uneasy. She *knew* she had left four apples. One was missing, and she didn't think a squirrel had carried away a big apple!

Jessie, however, began to work just as if nothing was wrong, She put an old copy of *Alice in Wonderland* in a box of what she thought might be more valuable books. The box was getting full.

"I'm tired!" Benny said after a while, sitting down on the floor and folding his arms. "I'm taking a rest!"

Violet sat in a chair. "That's a good idea." She took a deep breath. "I'm tired of books!"

"I think we all need a break," Henry said. "Let's bike down to the seashore."

"Perfect!" Jessie said. "First, though, let's set out our lunch. When we return we'll be starving."

Violet set one wrapped sandwich at each place, and Henry put three glasses and Benny's pink cup around the thermos in the middle of the big desk. Jessie put out napkins and the three apples. She didn't leave an apple at her place.

Happily they biked down to the coast. It was a two-mile ride, but they enjoyed it. The day was crisp, and the air salty.

Once at the shore, they all took off their shoes and ran along the sand. Then they waded in the cold water, laughing and splashing each other. White sea gulls dipped and soared above them. Benny found a crab, and Violet picked up three lovely shells. Two, of course, had a lavender tint. Henry and Jessie searched for interesting pieces of driftwood.

Everyone soaked up the sunshine for over an hour. Then, feeling refreshed, they headed back to the library.

Once inside, they eagerly sat down to eat.

Violet stared at her plate. It was empty. Finally she said in a low voice, "Someone has stolen my sandwich."

Benny, Jessie, and Henry looked at Violet's plate. Sure enough, the sandwich had disappeared.

Henry said nothing, but he glanced around him. Benny was right, he thought. There was a mysterious stranger in this library!

Violet moved closer to Jessie. "I don't like this one bit," she whispered, a worried frown on her face.

Jessie nodded her head. "Neither do I," she said. "The door was locked, yet someone was in here."

"Well," Henry said, breaking the silence. "There's only one thing to do. We'll need to search the upstairs."

Benny hung back. "Not me! I'm not going up there again!"

"Henry's right," Jessie said. "We have to find out who's up there."

Violet said weakly, "Yes, I guess you're right." But clearly she didn't want to.

CHAPTER 5

Miguel, the Runaway

Henry, his finger to his lips, loosened his laces and removed his sneakers. He motioned everyone else to do the same. Next, he tiptoed upstairs, the others following.

The Aldens searched upstairs, every corner, every nook, every cranny.

Jessie shrugged her slim shoulders. "There's no one here," she whispered.

Benny, who stood by the window, suddenly said in a loud, urgent whisper, "Henry, over here."

In four strides, Henry was at Benny's side. Benny pointed to the low velvet curtain below the window seat. Without a moment's hesitation, Henry yanked back the velvet seat covers.

There, huddled in a corner, was a small boy. His chin rested on his knees, and he stared at them with a frightened expression.

"Come out of there!" Henry said sternly. "Why are you hiding?"

"And why are you stealing our food?" Benny asked, his hands on his hips.

The frightened boy crawled out into the daylight. His face was thin and pale and a thatch of black hair fell forward on his forehead. He had the darkest brown eyes the Alden children had ever seen. He bowed his head. "I-I was hungry," he said softly.

"But why are you hiding?" Violet repeated. "We won't hurt you." Her voice was gentle.

"Before you answer any questions," Jessie said, "I think that you . . ." She stopped. "What's your name?"

"Miguel Morales," the boy answered

shyly. "I am ten years old." A proud gleam lighted his eyes.

"Well, Miguel," Jessie said kindly, "would you like a sandwich?"

Miguel nodded vigorously.

"I'm starved, too!" Benny said, rubbing his stomach.

They all laughed, going downstairs.

Over a sandwich and a glass of milk, Miguel told his story.

"I am hiding because," his voice caught in his throat, "because I heard two men at the bait shop in my town talking about how my father's fishing boat sank. They thought he and two other fishermen drowned. I ran before they could see me." Tears filled his eyes, and he put his sandwich down.

"When?" Jessie asked quietly.

"Two days ago." Miguel looked at each Alden. He knew they could be trusted. "You see, I live with my father in Dalton, which is many miles from here. My mother died three years ago, when I was seven."

"Poor Miguel," Violet sympathized. "How did you get here?"

He glanced at her gratefully and went on. "I walked for hours. Then I found this old building. I crawled through the back window."

"You scared me!" Benny said reproachfully.

"Sorry," Miguel mumbled. "I didn't mean to."

"So why are you hiding?" Henry asked.

"I have nowhere to go," Miguel said, a tear spilling down his cheek. "If my father drowned, I'll be put in a home."

"We won't let them!" Violet cried, her small chin jutting out. "We'll protect you. We know what it's like to have to hide from someone."

"Do we!" Benny said. "I'll never forget that old boxcar we lived in."

Violet nodded. "We don't have any parents, either, Miguel, and our grandfather was searching for us after our mother and father died. He planned to force us to live with him."

"We thought he was a mean man," Benny said.

Jessie smiled. "Grandfather Alden is just the opposite. He's very kind, and we have a wonderful home with him now. So you see something good can happen to you."

Sadly, Miguel shook his head.

"Yes, it will," Benny stated in a loud voice. "I know it will!"

Miguel looked up and gave them a weak smile. "Thanks, everyone. I know you won't turn me in."

"Well," Henry said slowly. "You can't stay here, Miguel. At least not forever." He smiled. "We'll do a little investigating. Maybe your father was rescued. Are you positive that he drowned?"

Miguel stared at Henry, his big eyes growing bigger. "I — I don't know," Miguel frowned. "I heard that *The Maria* sank and that three men drowned, and I ran."

"Your father's boat is called *The Maria*?" Jessie said.

Miguel nodded, unable to speak. Finally, he said, "My father named it after my mother."

"I see," Jessie said. She patted Miguel's

knee. "Whatever we decide you should do, we'll talk it over with you first. Is that okay?"

"That's okay," Miguel said, giving her a trembling smile.

"Then that's settled," Henry said. "Miguel, do you want to help us straighten books in this old library?"

"Oh, yes!" Miguel said eagerly. "I'm a good worker!"

And Miguel was as good as his word. He worked all afternoon, and when the sun set he was glad to go back to the house with his new friends. He sat behind Henry on his bicycle.

At supper Jessie smiled at Miguel. He was a good eater, like Benny. As she stacked the dirty dishes, she felt a sense of relief. At last the mystery was solved. No more strange noises, no more shadows, no more missing food.

CHAPTER 6

The Gray Glove

The next morning Henry biked to Pete's Café to buy milk and bread. But he had a more important reason. He needed to call Grandfather for advice.

Arriving at the café, Henry carefully placed his bike next to the white building. He entered the café and glanced around. Besides Pete there were only two other men, one at a table, and the other at the counter.

"Hi, Henry, my boy," Pete called. He was drinking a cup of coffee at the counter. "How do you like living in my house? Are you taking good care of it?"

Henry smiled. "We sure are." He liked old Pete. He'd been a friend of Grandfather's for years.

"I knew you kids would." Pete chuckled. "What brings you out so early, Henry?"

Henry smiled. "I need to buy bread and milk."

While Pete was taking the milk out of the refrigerator, Henry called Grandfather.

"Henry!" Grandfather Alden said in a delighted voice, "I'm glad to hear from you. Is everything all right?"

"Fine," Henry said, clearing his throat. "We found a small boy hiding in the library."

"Oh?" Grandfather said, waiting for Henry to continue.

"His name is Miguel Morales, and he's scared that he might be sent to a home. He's only ten, and he's all alone."

"Well," Grandfather began.

But Henry hurried on before Grandfather could interrupt. "You see Miguel's father was a fisherman, and his boat sank."

"Was it *The Maria*?"

"Yes," Henry said, surprised. "How did you know?"

"I heard the news on the radio. There were three fishermen on the boat."

"Yes, that's what Miguel said," Henry answered.

"I'll check with the Coast Guard and find out if anyone was rescued. Don't worry, Henry, we won't let Miguel be taken to a home."

Henry sighed with relief. Grandfather could always be depended upon to help.

"And what else have you been up to?" Grandfather Alden asked.

"Oh," Henry said. "I almost forgot. Benny discovered the hilt of a Civil War sword on the library shelves. We found a letter from General Meade awarding the sword to a Charles Howard. Captain Howard had been a courageous soldier at the Battle of Gettysburg."

"A Civil War sword!" Grandfather sounded excited. "That could be a very valuable find. Many museums would want to put it on display." He paused. "It could even help the library become a landmark. But didn't you find the rest of the sword?"

"No," Henry said. "Not yet. There are plenty of shelves, though, that we haven't cleaned. We might still find it."

"I hope it turns up," Grandfather said. "You've done a lot of work at the library. Are you and Violet and Jessie and Benny ready to come home?"

"Not yet," Henry said. "The library is getting clean and organized."

Grandfather chuckled. "All right, Henry. You take care. I'll be down next weekend to visit you. In the meantime, I want you all to bike in and have a good lunch at Pete's. And don't worry about the bill."

"Thanks, Grandfather. We'd like that! Good-bye. We'll see you soon." Henry turned back to Pete and was pleased that his groceries were already packed.

He pedaled back to the cabin. Benny was waiting outside.

"I'm thirsty," he complained.

"Why don't you drink a glass of water?" Henry teased.

Benny grinned, and his brown eyes sparkled. "You know what I'm thirsty for!"

"Oh!" Henry said, slapping his forehead. "I know what it is. It's cranberry juice!"

"No, it's not!" Benny shouted.

"Could it be this?" Henry asked as he lifted out a gallon carton of milk.

"Yes, yes," Benny said gleefully. "Is there bread, too?"

"Sure thing." Henry laughed as Benny held the door open for him.

Inside, they all had bread and milk. Everyone laughed at Miguel, who had a white rim of milk on his face. Miguel smiled, too. He liked his new friends.

"Is everyone ready to get to work?" Jessie asked.

"I am," Violet answered.

"So am I," Henry added.

"Me, too," Benny and Miguel echoed.

"Then let's get started," Jessie said with a smile. Her brown shiny hair was tied back with a blue ribbon.

* * *

Once in the library they rolled up their sleeves and started to work.

It wasn't long before Miguel let out a yell. "Look! This piece of metal was behind the books!" Triumphantly he held up part of the rusty sword.

Henry examined the long metal piece, then patted Miguel on the back. "This is the middle of our sword. Now we need to find the point of the blade, and our sword will be complete!"

"Hurrah for Miguel!" Benny shouted.

"Good for you, Miguel," Jessie said.

Violet patted Miguel's hand.

"It's almost time for lunch," Henry said. "We'll celebrate Miguel's find with a meal at Pete's."

Cheerfully they biked to the café. Henry had wrapped the sword part and placed it in his bicycle's basket. "I'm not letting this out of my sight!" he promised.

At Pete's Café, they ordered lobster, potatoes, salad, and apple pie à la mode. Pete was pleased to meet Miguel, the Aldens' new

friend. Since Miguel came from another town, Pete didn't recognize him. Pete was also pleased to see the children's good appetites.

Benny leaned back, patting his stomach. "That was a good lunch!"

Pete burst out laughing. "I've never seen such big eaters. You all deserve a treat."

Violet was puzzled. "Just for eating so much?" she questioned.

"No, just for being such nice children," Pete answered. "How would you like a ride in my fishing boat?"

"Oh, yes!" cried Benny. "I love to ride in a boat."

After they all boarded Captain Pete's red fishing boat, Pete started the motor, and they set off over the waves. The whitecaps slapped against the boat, sending the spray flying. Sometimes the water splashed over the sides of the boat.

They rode way out into the bay. When Benny shaded his eyes, he could barely see the café. It was only a white speck.

For over an hour the boat rode the waves.

Then Pete made a wide circle and headed back to the dock.

"That was fun!" Jessie said.

"Yes, sir!" Henry agreed, resting his hands on Benny's shoulders.

"Can we do it again?" Benny asked.

Pete chuckled. "Anytime, mates. Just let me know." He tied up the boat at the dock, and they jumped out.

Violet, the wind whipping through her long brown hair, said, "Thank you, Captain Pete."

"You're welcome, little lady," Pete answered. His wide grin lit up his wrinkled face.

"We'd like to take you up on your offer for another ride," Henry said. "We had a good time." He glanced at Miguel. "Did you have fun, Miguel?"

"Oh, yes," Miguel responded quietly, but he didn't look at Henry. Jessie noticed Miguel's sad, thin face.

"Miguel, we need to return to the library," Jessie said. She knew that Miguel was thinking of his father and the lost fishing boat. "Do you feel like working?"

He nodded. "I want to help," he said.

Except for Miguel, the Aldens mounted their bicycles. Miguel leapt up on the seat behind Henry, and they left for the library in high spirits.

Pushing open the library's door, they each went to the spot where they'd been working. Henry had filled one box with valuable books and was ready to start a second one.

Jessie hummed softly as she dusted off books. Suddenly, she stopped. "Look," she said in a low voice. From her fingertips she dangled a gray work glove.

Henry took the glove with black stitching around each finger. "This is a brand-new glove," he observed. "It's barely worn."

Jessie said, "Someone's been here . . . and left the glove."

Benny, Miguel, and Violet joined Henry and Jessie. No one said a word. Frightened, Benny glanced over his shoulder.

The mystery wasn't solved after all, Jessie thought. An intruder had invaded their library. A chill ran up her spine.

CHAPTER 7

The Strange Little Tune

Henry held up the gray glove and shrugged. "Someone was poking around in the library and forgot his glove, that's all. It's nothing to worry about." But secretly he wondered who it belonged to, and how the person had gotten in. He thought of the conversation he'd overheard in Pete's Café, but he didn't want to frighten the others by telling them.

Jessie smiled. "You're right, Henry. One glove doesn't mean a thing. Let's go back to the house and have a nice supper. We've done enough work today." She tried to sound unconcerned, but she was worried, too. Who was nearby?

Henry tucked the glove in his back pocket and threw his arm around his little brother. "What's the matter, Benny? You're not scared of an old glove, are you?"

Benny stood with his sturdy legs apart and his arms folded. "I'm not scared if you're not!"

"Atta, boy!" Henry said, tousling Benny's hair. He opened the door and stepped out into the setting sun. The others followed. The sun's rays gave the library a rosy glow. Carefully Henry locked the door, then twisted the knob to be sure that it was secure. It wouldn't be easy for an intruder to get in now!

That night the Aldens and Miguel ate peanut butter, crackers, and milk. They weren't very hungry after their big lobster lunch.

Benny and Miguel went to bed early.

"I'm filling the pitcher with fresh water," Jessie said, going out into the night. Darkness surrounded her.

As she pumped the water, Jessie suddenly stopped.

She heard a low humming.

She listened more closely, but the humming stopped. All she heard was the scuffling of an animal in the leaves.

All at once the low off-key humming started again. What a strange tune! This time she realized it was a person. Was someone watching her? Her pulse quickened. She wished Henry or Violet had come outside with her. "Henry," she called, then, "Violet," but her throat had tightened. All that came out was a croak.

The weird humming was loud and clear, but it soon faded. Jessie clutched the pitcher to her chest and raced toward the cabin. She stumbled on a branch, but kept running. The humming was very faint now. Fearfully, she glanced around. Was that a shadow moving up the path toward the library? Or was it her imagination?

With her heart pounding in her ears, she frantically threw open the door and flew into the room.

"What's wrong, Jessie?" Violet said, running to her side. "You're as white as your T-shirt."

"S-someone was humming a funny tune." She could barely get the words out as she set down the pitcher with a trembling hand. "I think I heard him going up the path toward the old library! I think I saw his shadow!"

Henry leapt up. "We'll see about this prowler!" he said angrily, grabbing the iron skillet from the stove and dashing outdoors. If he came upon the intruder, he wouldn't know what hit him! Bravely Henry silently stalked the stranger. Twice he circled the cabin, the skillet held high. Even though Jessie had said she'd seen the prowler going toward the library, Henry carefully investigated around the house. Then he ran a short way up the gravel path, but didn't see anyone. Not even Jessie's imagined shadow. Nor did he hear anything. The humming had stopped. He listened intently, but all he heard was the breeze rustling through the trees.

He returned to the house. "I didn't hear

anything, Jessie. Maybe it was the hum of an insect."

Jessie shook her head. "No," she said positively. "It was *someone* humming! And the person was nearby, watching me. Then the humming grew faint. I saw his outline as he went toward the library." She poured a glass of water for her dry throat and turned her big brown eyes on Henry. "I'm certain he's after something!"

"I think I know what it is," Henry said thoughtfully. "When I called Grandfather, I told him about the piece of sword we'd found. Anyone could have overheard me. But don't worry," he said in a confident tone. "The sword is always with me! At night it's under my pillow, and during the day I take it with me on my bike. The sword is wrapped so no one can see what it is."

Quickly he told Violet and Jessie about the two men he'd overheard in Pete's Café. "But whoever that thief is can't be our guy. How would he know about the sword?" He spoke in a low voice so as not to wake Benny and Miguel.

"He couldn't," Jessie added.

"What should we do?" Violet asked. "Is it safe to stay here? I hate to leave until we finish at the library."

"Then we won't leave!" Jessie said in a firm voice. There was a stubborn gleam in her dark eyes. "We have to find the third part of the sword. Once we find it, we'll go home."

"You're right!" Violet said with a tight little smile. "No one can drive us away after we've worked hard and found the sword. The sword is ours!"

They went to bed, and Jessie pulled the blanket up to her chin. Even though everything was silent, she could still hear that awful weird tune in her head.

The next morning the sun washed their fears away.

Henry ate an early breakfast, then scraped back his chair and stood up. "I'm going to make a quick trip to the marina and phone Grandfather," he said to Jessie.

"Do you think he'll have any news about Miguel's father?"

"I hope so. Grandfather was going to contact the Coast Guard."

On his way to the café, without warning, the sun dipped behind the clouds. The sky became a gloomy gray. Henry pedaled faster when he heard a low rumble of distant thunder.

Entering Pete's Café, Henry saw Pete at the counter pouring a cup of coffee for a customer. He looked up at Henry's entrance. "Hi, Henry! Feel like a boat ride?"

"Not today." Henry smiled.

Old Pete chuckled. "You show good sense, boy." He pointed to the large window and the ocean beyond. "Look at those waves!"

Henry watched the waves pound against the stone pier. The whitecaps rolled in, churning toward the shore and ending in foamy puddles. The sky was almost black with the wind blowing from the north. The thunder boomed.

"Yup," Pete said. "Even the Coast Guard won't come out in this weather."

Henry excused himself to phone Grandfather Alden.

After a few rings, Grandfather's warm voice came on the line. "Henry! I'm glad you called. I contacted the Coast Guard, and they informed me that two fishermen were rescued from *The Maria*."

"Only two?" Henry asked, and his heart sank.

"Yes, I'm afraid the third man drowned," Grandfather said gravely.

"Was it Miguel's father?" Henry asked, dreading to hear the answer.

"They won't give out the names of the men until all the families are notified. The survivors are on Bear Island and as soon as the storm lets up, they'll be brought to Pete's marina."

"Thanks, Grandfather."

"Depending on the weather, I'll be down to see you on Friday."

"That will be great, Grandfather," Henry said. "Everyone wants to see you."

"Good, good," Grandfather said.

Henry said good-bye. After exchanging a few words with Pete, he biked back to the house. He hated to tell Miguel about the one drowned fisherman, but he had a right to know. After all, his father *could* be one of the rescued men.

Entering the cabin, Henry sat down at the table next to Miguel. He quietly told him that only two men had been rescued.

Miguel stared at him, biting his lower lip. "Wh-what were the names of the two fishermen?" he whispered.

"No names have been released yet," said Henry, reaching out and putting a hand on Miguel's shoulder. "Until this storm subsides, the rescued men will stay at the Coast Guard station on Bear Island." A stab of lightning lit up the room.

Jessie stood behind Miguel. "It will be all right," she soothed. "I'm certain one of the men will be your father."

Miguel glanced back at her. "But what if he isn't?" he said in a trembling voice. "My father knew how to swim, but what good is that in a stormy sea?" His lips tightened, and his body was rigid. He tried not to cry.

"He had a life preserver, didn't he?" asked Violet, coming from the kitchen and sitting down. Her voice was soft, and her eyes were filled with compassion.

"He had a life preserver, but . . ." his voice faltered. "Oh, I don't know what to think." Miguel lowered his eyes. His small face twisted with pain. "What if he drowned? My poor father. I-I love him."

"No matter what happens," Henry said, "we'll stick by you!"

"You bet we will!" Benny echoed, standing in the doorway. He frowned, and his eyes were sad. All at once his face brightened. "I know your dad was saved. I feel it in my bones!"

Miguel smiled at Benny. "Thanks, Benny. Thanks, everyone! I know you all hope for the best." But his heart thudded against his ribs. He had a feeling that his father was gone, and he'd never see him again. He jumped up and turned his back on his friends. How could he repay the Aldens' kindness? He couldn't stay with them forever. He made up his mind. If he heard bad news, he'd run away. He'd have to be on his own again. His heartbeat matched the thunder that rolled outside!

CHAPTER 8

The Locked Door

That afternoon it was so windy the Aldens left their bikes at home. They each struggled against the ferocious wind to reach the library. Violet and Miguel held Benny's hands. Henry, leaning against the wind, was the first to the library. He unlocked the door and pushed his way in. The other children followed.

"Whew, what a storm," Jessie said, collapsing in a chair. "I need a rest."

"Me, too," Violet agreed.

"Not me!" Benny said. "I'm ready to work!"

Henry laughed as he removed his rain jacket. "It's no wonder you're ready to work, Benny. You had a little help in fighting the storm!"

"I know." Benny grinned impishly. "You look tired. Go and rest, Henry, and I'll straighten a pile of books."

"You do that," Henry said. "But I'll be working!" He peered at the nearest shelf. To his astonishment, he saw very fresh fingerprints. Could they belong to the person Jessie had heard humming the night before?

Casually, Henry piled books over the telltale prints. There was no sense in alarming everyone, he thought. Why was someone searching the library? Was he looking for the sword?

He turned around and faced his sisters and Miguel. "Let's work especially hard today and try to find the missing sword point. I think we're all ready to go home."

"Not until we find the *whole* sword, though," Benny shouted as he came racing downstairs. He smiled at Violet and Jessie. "Right?"

"Right," Jessie answered, laughing at Benny's determination.

"And I don't want to quit, either," Miguel said, stepping forward. "Until I find out what happened to my father, I'll stay and help everyone. You've been kind to me." He smiled.

"Good!" exclaimed Henry. "We're kind to you because you're a splendid fellow, Miguel."

Miguel felt safe and secure with the Aldens. He wished he would never have to leave.

For a moment, no one said a word. Their hearts went out to Miguel.

Henry broke the silence. "I'll work upstairs and sort through the books."

"May I go with you?" Benny asked. "I can help you, Henry."

"I'm sure you can," Henry said with a chuckle.

All afternoon they worked — Benny and Henry upstairs, and Violet, Jessie, and Miguel downstairs. Almost every bookshelf was neat and clean. The books were upright on the shelves, but not a clue turned up as to where the sword point could be.

Finally, Jessie stopped. She glanced at the rattling windows and the rain pelting against the glass panes. "I'm ready to go home," she said. "Are you, Violet?"

Violet rose to her feet, several volumes in her hand. Her face was smudged, and her shirt wrinkled. "Yes," she said. "I'm more than ready."

"Did I hear someone say they wanted to go back to the house?" Henry questioned. "In this rain?"

"I don't care how wet I get," Benny said, dragging himself down the steps. "I'm hungry and tired, and I want to go home."

"Shall we make a run for it?" Henry asked. "If we do, we'll get soaked."

"It doesn't matter," Jessie replied. "I don't want to stay in this library all night." She flung her blue coat over her shoulders. "Just think! The person I heard humming might stay here at night."

Henry gave her a sharp look, but soon realized she hadn't seen the new fingerprints.

He helped Benny with his red raincoat, then struggled into his own.

Violet buttoned her lavender raincoat but propped her purple umbrella by the door. There was no sense in letting the wind whip it inside out. Miguel wore a yellow slicker, just like a fisherman, which he had hidden under the window seat.

"Okay," Henry yelled. "Let's run all the way to the house."

With a whoop, Benny was the first to rush out the door. The raindrops fell faster now, but Benny didn't care. He lifted his head to the rain, enjoying the fresh drops on his face.

"I'll race you!" he challenged, but his words were lost in the roar of the wind. Benny raced down the path. All that could be seen below his red rain gear were his sneakers.

Everyone ran through the mud and the rain. When they reached the house, Benny splashed about in a mud puddle. "Let's stay outside and play in the rain."

"Not a chance," Jessie said, shivering from the wet cold.

"I thought you were tired," Violet said to Benny softly, her eyes twinkling.

"I was," Benny said. "The rain made me awake! It was fun!"

Miguel, drops of water glistening on his long lashes, laughed, too. "It was fun, wasn't it?"

"All right, you two. Time to remove your wet things. Go upstairs and get into your dry pajamas," Jessie ordered with a smile.

"Okay, Jessie." And Benny was upstairs before Henry had his coat off.

Jessie built a blazing fire in the fireplace while everyone changed into warm dry clothes.

Henry, in jeans and a sweater, and Violet, in a violet blouse and jeans, took the leftover soup out of the refrigerator and set it on the stove.

While the soup was simmering, everyone drank hot apple cider and sat before the fireplace. They felt cozy and warm as they watched the orange flames.

In the morning, feeling refreshed after a

good night's sleep, they had hot cereal, but-tered toast, and cocoa for breakfast, and were ready for a day at the library. Maybe today they would find the rest of the sword. The wind still howled, but the rain had stopped.

"Do you think the Coast Guard will bring in the two fishermen today?" Miguel asked in a low tone, barely above a whisper. His father was always in his thoughts.

Henry glanced out the window at the gray sky and the swaying tree branches. "Not to-day, Miguel. The wind isn't as bad as yes-terday, but the ocean waves are too high. I'm sure, though, your father will be found safe and sound in a day or two."

Miguel met Henry's eyes and his voice was husky. "I wish I were as certain as you that he's alive. I pray you're right!"

Benny piped up, changing the subject. "That was a good breakfast." He jumped up and ran to the door. "I want to see how windy it is."

"Careful you're not blown over," Henry teased.

Benny tried to open the door, but it

wouldn't budge. He leaned against it with his shoulder and shoved as hard as he could. The door was stuck fast!

"Henry," Benny panted. "The door won't open!"

Henry laughed. "The wind is strong, Benny, but I don't think it's that strong." He turned the handle and pushed against the door, but Henry couldn't open it, either. He pushed three times, but the door remained shut.

"Let's all try," Jessie suggested. All five put their shoulders to the door, but it remained closed.

Puzzled, Henry shook his head. "Maybe something has blown in front of the door and jammed it shut."

"I don't think so," Jessie said. Worry lines creased her forehead.

"I need to check the door from the outside," Henry said, "but I have a problem." He stared at the narrow windows. "The windows are too small. I can't squeeze through."

"I could!" Benny shouted. "Let me! Let me!"

Henry nodded. "Okay, Benny, you're the only one small enough to crawl through."

Henry opened a window and lifted Benny up. Benny wiggled through the narrow opening and dropped to the ground.

Benny hurried around the cabin to the front door. There, to his surprise, was a heavy branch shoved through the door handle. No wonder it wouldn't turn. He tugged with all his might and was able to pull the branch out. "You can open the door now," he yelled.

Henry opened the door, and Benny showed him the branch that had locked them in.

"Someone deliberately tried to keep us from getting out, didn't they?" Violet asked.

"I'm afraid so," Henry answered.

Jessie's throat tightened, and her mouth was dry. Was someone trying to keep them from getting to the library? She pulled her sweater tighter around her. What would they find when they reached the library?

CHAPTER 9

The Upside-down Mess

The day before, the Aldens and Miguel had run up the rain-splashed path, not minding the wet and cold. This morning, however, after they had escaped the house's bolted door, they walked up the path to the library without a word. They all were worrying about who had tried to keep them in Pete's house.

Henry took out the library key to unlock the door, but as he came closer, he noticed the door was ajar.

He hesitated. "Someone might be in there.

Keep a sharp lookout," he advised.

"D-do you think we should go in?" Violet asked timidly.

"We've worked very hard," Henry said calmly. "Do you want to stop now?"

"No," Jessie said. "Let's just look in."

Henry pushed the door open. He listened carefully for any sounds. When he heard nothing, he stepped inside. The others followed, peering around.

Entering the library, Jessie stopped. Her hand flew to her mouth at the sight that greeted her. "Oh, no," she wailed. "Look at this mess!"

Violet was behind her. "Who would do such a thing?" she asked in a shocked voice.

Miguel's face paled. "The books are scattered everywhere!" He stepped over a stack of books. "Look! The desk is upside down."

Books were upside down, too. Books were right side up, standing on end, and tossed in corners. Leaves of books had been ripped out and cast here and there. Some pages had been crumpled, others torn to shreds. There was no doubt about it! Someone had locked them

in Pete's house to gain time to search. The books, the shelves, and every nook had been explored.

"All our hard work is wasted!" Violet said.

Speechless, Henry stood with his hands on his hips, shaking his head in disbelief. He picked up a tattered book.

Benny gazed at Henry. "This is bad, isn't it?"

Henry paused, then spoke in a calm manner. "It's bad, Benny, but nothing that can't be fixed. Books are everywhere, but there's no major damage."

Jessie rose. "We'll need to put the books back on the shelf, that's all." She rolled up her sleeves.

Miguel held up a book, studying it curiously. "Where did these jagged holes come from?"

Henry reached for the book and examined the pages. "Our prowler," he observed, "has done this on purpose! He's used scissors to slash these books!"

"Who would do such a terrible thing?" asked Miguel.

"Someone who is angry because he can't find what he wants," Jessie answered. Her eyebrows knit together in a frown. "The intruder not only balled up pages and tossed them aside, but stabbed the bigger books with his scissors or a knife!"

"What a shame," Violet said. "He must have been furious when he didn't find what he was hunting for."

"I need to check upstairs and see how many books have been ruined up there," Henry said.

Jessie moved to his side. She anxiously chewed on her underlip. "Grandfather will be so disappointed if the library isn't a landmark."

Henry smiled grimly. "I know, Jessie. It's pretty discouraging, but we'll clean up this mess." He wheeled about and hurried upstairs.

Soon Henry returned. "Good news! The upstairs has hardly been touched. The intruder only tore apart one shelf."

Violet tilted her head. "We must have interrupted whoever it was," she said thoughtfully.

"You're right, Violet," Jessie said. "When he heard us coming, he must have dashed out the backdoor."

"Do you think the awful person will come back?" Benny asked. His brown eyes were big.

"He probably will, Benny. He wants that sword! I'm sure of it." Henry tossed a ruined book on top of the damaged pile.

"Do you think we should call the police?" Violet asked.

"There's no phone here or in the cabin," Henry said. "Let's wait. The police would probably want us to stay out of the library."

For the rest of the day they tackled the books. Book after book was put back on the shelves. Others were stacked neatly in piles.

By the end of the day the floor had been cleared. Jessie had collected the damaged books in a box. Henry had swept the floor of all the torn pages and debris.

Miguel leaned backward, then forward. "My back hurts," he complained with a smile. "I feel good, though. Look how much we've done!"

Henry smiled at Miguel, placing a hand on his shoulder. "I don't know what we'd have done without you!"

Miguel grinned, happy to be needed.

"I'll lock the door," Henry said, "but I'm not sure it will keep out the stranger. I'm willing to bet he has a passkey. He *must* have."

They left for the house, tired and discouraged. Henry kept his thoughts to himself, but certain questions ran through his mind. What if they returned tomorrow and the books were topsy-turvy again? How could they go through all this work another time? Someone seemed to know their every move. And what if that someone found the missing sword piece before they did? And what if he *didn't*? If the intruder was desperate enough for the sword, there was no telling what he might do!

Jessie caught up with Henry. "At least the intruder didn't find what he was searching for."

"No, Jessie," Henry responded. "But I'm afraid he might become dangerous." He frowned. "Maybe we'd better pack up and go home."

"We've come this far," Jessie said softly. "We mustn't give up now!"

Henry gave her a grateful glance. "I was hoping you'd say that!" He patted his back pocket. "The letter is with me all the time, and the sword is either under my pillow or on my bike or in the library when I'm working."

Violet lagged behind, picking wildflowers. She loved flowers, especially violet ones. The others were far ahead, and the sun was setting. She felt uneasy. She'd better catch up with everyone. All at once she heard a faint noise in back of her. Someone was following her! Heavy steps on the pebble path made a crunching noise. She whirled about. A shadowy figure dived into the shrubs. Violet raced toward the others. "Henry!" she called. "Wait!"

They stopped. "What is it, Violet?" Henry asked.

"A man! I saw a man duck into the bushes." She was out of breath, but felt better surrounded by her family and Miguel.

"Don't worry!" Benny said. "We'll protect you!"

Henry chuckled nervously. "We've almost reached the house. We'll be safe there." But his heart was racing, too. One more day, he vowed, and they must leave! Things were getting out of hand!

That night no one slept well.

Benny thrashed about in bed and pounded his pillow. Then he lay very still. What was that click? But it was only his chattering teeth.

Miguel thought he heard the stranger trying to break in, but it was only the branches scraping against the window.

Henry thought he heard a scratching noise, but it was only a mouse.

Jessie thought she heard someone breaking the lock, but it was only the dying embers in the fireplace that crackled and popped.

Violet sat straight up in bed. Was someone ripping and tearing something? No, she thought, lying back. It was probably her imagination again.

CHAPTER 10

The Last Missing Piece

When dawn broke, Henry awakened and jumped out of bed. Quietly he went into the kitchen. Jessie joined him. Then Violet and Miguel came in.

And last, Benny slowly shuffled toward them. He gave a wide yawn and rubbed his half-closed eyes. "Is it time to get up?" he asked sleepily.

"No," Henry said. "I couldn't sleep."

"Neither could I," Jessie said.

"Me neither," Violet echoed.

"I woke up lots of times," Miguel said.

"I didn't sleep very good either!" Benny said.

In the half light Henry moved toward the fireplace. Suddenly he halted, unable to go another step.

Jessie, who was beside him, stopped also. "The chair!" she exclaimed. "It's ripped to shreds."

"So it wasn't my imagination after all," Violet said in a husky voice, a hand flying to her flushed cheek. "To think the intruder was in the *house* while we were sleeping!" She shivered, hating to think how near a stranger had been.

"Well," Henry said, trying to laugh, "it looks like Pete has one ruined chair."

"I'll say," Benny said in a low tone. "The chair is all stuffing and springs."

They stared at the damage, not quite knowing how to handle this.

Jessie was the first to stir. She forced a cheerful smile. "There's not much we can do about the damage." She hesitated, then continued, "Besides, that old chair was so caved in that you almost sank to the floor."

"Oh, Pete won't care. It's just the thought of someone . . ." Henry didn't finish.

"Someone being so close," Miguel finished.

"Right," Violet said. Her face was pale. "Shall we go for help?"

Jessie, attempting to keep her smile, said, "If word gets out there's a prowler, we won't be able to finish."

Henry nodded. "We'll be very careful. We have to keep our eyes open every minute, and we have to stay together."

"Will he come back tonight?" Benny asked in a small frightened voice, his eyes fastened on Henry's face.

They all shifted their feet uneasily, but Henry was positive. "Absolutely not! We only have one more night here, and we'll take turns standing guard. We'll work in the library today and if we don't find the missing sword, then I guess it will never be found!"

Jessie leaned down, looking at Benny. "You must eat some breakfast, Benny."

Benny shook his head.

"I can't believe you're not hungry," Miguel

said with concern in his dark eyes. "You must eat so you can help at the library."

"I'm tired of working in the library."

"Then you can be our lookout today," Henry said. "You won't have to lift books anymore."

"Really?" he said, slowly weakening.

"Yes," Jessie said.

Benny stared at Jessie with his big brown eyes. "Can we have pancakes?" He smiled impishly.

Violet laughed. "That's just the breakfast I was thinking of," she said.

"Then, I guess I'm hungry, after all," Benny said, going into the kitchen.

They all pitched in, making the morning meal. Henry set the table, Jessie made the pancakes, Violet poured the milk, and Miguel set the syrup and butter on the table. Benny folded napkins and set one at each place, but every once in a while he stopped and glanced at the ruined chair.

Everyone ate a hearty breakfast, trying to forget the intruder who had been in their house.

They decided to bike to the library and on the way Henry began to sing, and soon everyone joined in. In the bright sunlight, the stranger didn't seem so ominous. Besides, it was their last day, and tonight the lookout would warn them if anyone approached the little house.

When they reached the library, Henry paused before opening the door. What if it was a mess again? He shook his head to get rid of the awful picture of yesterday's chaos, and flung open the door.

All was as they had left it yesterday. Everyone crowded behind Henry, peeking over his shoulder.

"It's all right," he laughed. "You can come in."

Row after row of books lined the shelves. Boxes of books, tied with string and labeled, hadn't been opened.

"Wow," Benny exclaimed. He beamed his approval.

"Doesn't everything look grand?" Henry said, surveying the room with his hands on his hips.

Jessie stood beside him. "All our hard work has paid off."

"Wait until Grandfather sees how lovely the library looks," Violet said with a sweet smile.

"What's the matter, Miguel?" Henry motioned the boy forward. "You helped in this, too, you know."

"It's the nicest library I've ever seen," Miguel said, but he still hung back.

Jessie and Violet exchanged glances. They knew why he wasn't in a happy mood. The wind had died down, and now Miguel would have to face the two fishermen who would soon be brought to shore. Miguel might be the happiest boy in the world or the most heartbroken. Jessie took Miguel's hand, pulling him into the group.

"We only have the upstairs and we'll be finished," Henry said briskly, attempting to distract Miguel so he wouldn't think too much.

"There aren't many books upstairs," Jessie said lightly, already mounting the steps.

"Now, Benny," Henry said gravely. "You

stay downstairs and be our guard. If anyone approaches, you yell a warning."

"Okay," Benny said, feeling important. He climbed atop the circulation desk. "I'll sit right here and look out the window," he said, swinging his legs.

"Good boy," Henry said. "We don't need to worry with you as our lookout."

"You bet you don't!" Benny grinned, glad not to have to handle any more books. Being a guard was much easier.

Violet patted Benny's knee. "We shouldn't be too long."

"That's okay," Benny answered, resting his chin in his hand and staring intently out the window.

Henry, Violet, and Miguel went upstairs where Jessie was already straightening books.

After two hours of hard work, their job was almost ended.

Suddenly they heard a thud. Then another.

"What was that?" Violet asked in a shaky voice.

Henry laughed. "Did you see the rubber ball sticking out of Benny's back pocket?"

"Oh, is that it?" Violet said in relief, listening to the steady bounce of the ball.

All at once the noise stopped.

They all listened.

Benny shouted, "Hurry, hurry! See what I've found."

They rushed downstairs.

Benny, bending over a hole in the floor, pulled and tugged at something below the floorboards.

"What is it, Benny?" Jessie questioned, her brown eyes sparkling with curiosity.

"I was playing with the ball, and it rolled into the hole," Benny panted. His face was beet-red, and he grunted with huge effort. He gave one final pull and lifted out a rusty black object.

"What in the world did you find?" Violet asked.

"It looks like the point of the sword," Miguel said.

Jessie eagerly seized the metal from Benny. "*It is!*" she cried triumphantly. "It's the missing sword piece! Now our Civil War sword is complete!"

Henry said slowly, "I hope we can get it home without the stranger finding out."

Just then the back door slammed.

Benny jumped.

Everyone's eyes darted from one to the other.

"Is it the prowler?" Jessie whispered.

"Nonsense!" Henry said with a snort. He ran to the back door and quickly returned. "Not a soul in sight. It was only the wind," he said heartily. But there was doubt written all over his face.

The others were doubtful, too.

"How come the backdoor wasn't locked?" Violet asked.

Benny looked sheepish. "I opened it before to look outside."

Henry sighed. "Remember I said we have to be careful . . . very careful."

CHAPTER 11

The Prowler

"We're leaving!" Henry said. "We're heading back to the house." He carefully wrapped the point of the sword in a dust rag. "No telling who's around here."

"I thought you said it was only the wind that slammed the door," Benny said, his head tilted to one side.

"It probably was," Jessie soothed.

Henry gave a last look at the tidy library — so different from when they'd first entered — then locked the door.

With the prowler on their minds, everyone hastily mounted their bicycles. As fast as they could, they biked back to Pete's house. Benny's legs had never pushed so hard.

Back in the house, however, they tried to forget the slammed door. Maybe it was the wind, maybe it was the prowler spying on them, but whatever it was, they were safe and sound now.

"One more night!" Benny crowed. "And Grandfather will be here. He'll be proud we found the rest of the sword!"

"Thanks to you," Jessie said, giving his hand a squeeze.

"Just think," Violet said happily. "Tomorrow we'll be going home."

"Yes, but we still have tonight to get through," Miguel said gloomily.

"No problem," Henry said. He was worried about Miguel, though. The slim boy was so sad. It wouldn't be long before he knew whether his father was alive or not. "Miguel, why don't you help me chop wood?" Henry asked. "We'll leave a nice stack for Pete."

At supper they lingered over their spaghetti and meatballs, enjoying their last night in Pete's house.

When they'd finished eating, Henry fit the sword together on a braided rug before the fireplace. Even though the blade was rusty and black, it was graceful and beautiful.

"I can imagine how the sword will look when it's polished. The silver and gold will gleam," Jessie said, admiring it.

"Such a wonderful sword," Violet said. "Captain Howard must have been very proud to have been honored with such a gift."

"The Civil War was over one hundred years ago," Jessie said thoughtfully. "I wonder what happened to Captain Howard."

Henry, busy polishing the hilt, said, "Oh, he probably retired to his farm near Gettysburg and lived to a ripe old age."

"What makes you think the Captain was from Pennsylvania?" Miguel asked.

Henry shrugged. "Just a guess. He may not have been."

"I'll bet he looked handsome in his uniform," Jessie said, gazing at the sword.

Henry chuckled. "You've got a vivid imagination, Jessie."

Jessie laughed. "I'm not the artistic one." She glanced at Violet. "Violet is."

Violet's cheeks grew pink. She did love music and her violin, and she did enjoy painting.

"Time for bed, everybody!" Henry said. "The earlier we go to bed, the earlier we'll get up. Grandfather said he'd visit us tomorrow, and if I know him, he'll be here for breakfast."

"We need to leave Pete's house spick-and-span, too," Jessie said. "Pete will be glad for the wood you left him, Henry."

Henry nodded. "And I'm certain he'll be pleased when he sees how clean the windows and floors are."

"I hope so," Jessie said.

"I'm sure he will," Violet said, smiling at Jessie. They had really worked while on their adventure, but now that it was almost over, they felt good.

Jessie picked up the pitcher. "I'm going out to fill this with water," she said. "I know Benny will want a drink before he goes to sleep."

"You're not afraid, are you?" Violet asked. "Maybe the hummer will be outside waiting for you."

Jessie laughed. "I'm not frightened at all." She moved to the door. "Besides, I'll only be gone five minutes."

After Jessie left, Benny and Miguel went to bed while Violet set the table for breakfast. She smiled as she set a place for Grandfather.

Henry carefully rewrapped the sword in the dust rag and waited for Jessie's return.

Outdoors, Jessie stepped quickly to the pump. She didn't intend to tarry any longer than necessary.

"Hooo, hooo," came a strange call from the trees.

Jessie halted, listening intently.

"Hoooo, hooo."

She stared at the large oak. Then a smile broke over her face. The yellow unblinking eyes of an owl stared back at her.

"Go ahead and hoot, Mr. Owl," Jessie said as she pumped fresh cold spring water. "I'm not afraid."

A twig snapped, but Jessie kept pumping as if she hadn't heard a thing.

Footsteps approached. Jessie froze. The stranger was back again! A cold chill ran up her spine.

All at once she whirled about, flinging the pitcher in the air. She'd almost reached the door when a cloth bag was thrown over her head, blotting out sight and air. Her arms were pinned to her side.

"Henry!" she screamed, but her muffled voice was lost in the cloth. She struggled for a breath of air.

"The sword is mine!" the stranger growled in her ear. "Get out!"

Jessie's heart thumped against her ribs, but she knew what to do.

"Do you understand me?" The prowler growled menacingly.

Suddenly, Jessie kicked the man's shins hard, and he let go of her arms to grab his painful legs. She yanked off the bag and gulped in air. She yelled, "Help! Help!"

Yellow light streamed from the house as Henry tore open the door.

"The prowler!" she shouted, pointing at a

shadowy figure disappearing in the brush.

The bushes violently swayed back and forth. An instant later a car's engine started, and the intruder sped away.

Henry dashed to Jessie's side. "Are you all right?" he asked with concern, throwing his arms around her.

She nodded numbly, glad for Henry's warmth. The water pitcher was forgotten as they hurried into the house.

"Jessie!" Violet said, rushing to her side.

Once inside, Henry bolted the door. Jessie sank down before the fire with Violet beside her. Henry brought her a glass of orange juice.

"H-he told us to get out! That the sword was his!" Jessie shuddered. "That awful, awful man! He almost smothered me! If I hadn't kicked him hard, I wouldn't have escaped!"

"It's over," Henry said softly. "He's far away by now!" But his heart was beating rapidly when he glanced at Jessie's white face. He wondered if the locked door could keep out such a determined stranger!

CHAPTER 12

What Did Benny See?

That night, while Henry stood guard, everyone was restless. Jessie heard a barking dog, Violet heard an owl hoot, Benny heard a scolding squirrel, and Miguel heard the wind in the trees. The children tossed and turned all night, sitting up in bed at each sound they heard.

In the morning, though, when the sun peeped through the window, they jumped out of bed, eager to greet their grandfather and go home.

"I can't wait to see Grandfather," Violet

said, strapping on her watch. "It's almost nine o'clock."

"I can't, either," Jessie said, smiling at her sister.

"I hear someone in the kitchen already," Violet said.

"It's Henry. He promised to fill the pitcher with water." Jessie laughed. "If he can find it after I threw it in the brush!"

Laughing, the girls went into the kitchen. Sure enough, Henry was setting out the glasses.

Soon Miguel and Benny woke up.

"Good morning, Miguel," Violet said.

Miguel barely nodded. " 'Morning," he mumbled.

"Come sit down," Jessie said, pouring his orange juice. "You look upset." Her eyes were sympathetic.

"Yes," Miguel said in a low tone, sliding into his chair but not drinking his juice. "Today I'll find out about my father."

"Don't worry," Jessie said gently. "I know it will be okay."

Miguel smiled weakly. "I hope so," he said.

"Here's the water," Henry said, putting the pitcher on the counter. He laughed. "I had to search in every bush." He winked at Jessie. "You've got a strong arm."

"Yes," Jessie said, smiling. "Last night, my strong foot could have saved my life."

Henry stopped smiling. "I'm glad you're so quick!"

Benny, who sat by the window, said, "I see a big car coming around the curve." He leapt down. "It's Grandfather!" he shouted.

Henry opened the door, and they all ran out to greet him.

When his car pulled up, Benny dashed forward. "Grandfather! We've been waiting for you!"

Grandfather Alden picked up Benny and swung him around. Then everyone crowded around, hugging and kissing. All, that is, except the sad boy in the background.

"Is this Miguel?" Grandfather Alden asked kindly.

"Yes," Miguel answered shyly, moving forward and shaking Grandfather's hand. "I'm Miguel Morales."

"Well, my boy," Grandfather said, "the Coast Guard is bringing in the two fishermen today."

"They are?" Miguel said, his mouth so dry he could barely speak.

"We'll drive down to Pete's Café after breakfast," Grandfather promised.

Miguel nodded stiffly. He was uncertain if he really wanted to go.

"How's Watch?" Jessie asked.

"Watch is eagerly waiting for you," Grandfather replied, "but the dog and I got along fine."

"Good," Jessie said, obviously glad Watch had been taken good care of. "And now," she announced, "it's time to eat."

"We're having Benny's favorite blueberry pancakes in honor of our last day here," Violet said.

"Well, well," Grandfather laughed heartily. "Think of that. Blueberry pancakes are my favorite, too!"

"I know." Benny grinned.

Jessie set a pile of pancakes on the table, and Violet poured the milk.

Benny wiggled in his chair. He was so excited, he couldn't sit still.

While they ate, Grandfather heard all about the library and the sword and the mysterious stranger. He frowned when he realized how close to danger his grandchildren and Miguel had been. The sooner they left, the better!

After the breakfast dishes were washed, everyone packed his or her belongings.

Grandfather glanced around the room. "Pete has a nice house. Clean and cozy." His blue eyes twinkled. "I'm sure you all had something to do with the way it looks."

"It was fun," Jessie said, then added softly, "except for the stranger."

Grandfather's eyes grew serious. "Well, we'll be leaving soon, and you'll be safe."

"Look, Grandfather," Henry said, fitting the sword pieces together on the table.

"It's magnificent!" Grandfather exclaimed. He ran his fingers lightly over the blade. "No wonder someone is after this valuable sword!"

"The sword was awarded to Captain

Charles Howard," Violet explained.

"Yes," Jessie continued, "because of his bravery at the Battle of Gettysburg."

"My, my," Grandfather said in wonder as he stroked his chin. "Wouldn't a museum be glad to have this!"

"It's beautiful," Miguel said.

Grandfather turned to the slim, shy boy. "I know you must be anxious to go to Pete's Café."

"Y-yes," Miguel stammered. "I guess I am."

"Then," Grandfather directed, "Henry, wrap up the sword, and we'll put it in the trunk of the car . . . and don't forget your bikes, too. Let's get going!"

"Great idea," Henry agreed, carefully wrapping the three pieces individually.

Once in the car, no one said a word for the whole two miles. Everyone's thoughts were of Miguel. Everyone hoped his father would be alive.

Arriving at the marina, they jumped out of the car.

Waving, Pete came out to greet them.

"Hello, Aldens!" He shook Grandfather's hand. "How are you, James?"

"Fine, Pete, just fine," Grandfather said, looking around. "But where are the two fishermen?"

Pete jerked a thumb over his shoulder. "Inside, drinking coffee."

Miguel slipped past Grandfather and dashed into the café.

The others hurried in behind him. Jessie held her breath.

Miguel searched the room. Suddenly he let out a yell. "Father!" He rushed into the arms of a man who had jumped up from a back booth.

"My son," the man cried. For a moment all was silent, as father and son clung to one another.

"Father," Miguel said, "I was worried. I'm so glad you're safe."

"Yes, I'm lucky," his father answered. Even though the man smiled, tears glistened in his eyes. He ran a trembling hand over Miguel's thick hair. "Poor Joseph drowned."

"I-I was afraid it was you," Miguel whis-

pered, hugging his father even tighter.

Grandfather moved to Miguel's side. "We're happy for you, Miguel." The Alden children joined him and grabbed Miguel's hand.

Miguel broke away, remembering his manners. "This is my father, Pedro Morales." He introduced Mr. Alden, Jessie, Violet, Henry, and Benny.

"Thank you," Pedro said, with shining eyes. "You took good care of my son."

"Hurray for Mr. Morales!" Benny shouted. "Hurray for Miguel!" Suddenly his smile vanished as he listened to something and turned to stare at the man at the counter. He moved to Henry's side. "Look! Look over there," he whispered. "That man's humming a funny tune. Maybe it's the man Jessie heard." He shivered, reaching for Violet's hand. "I'm afraid."

CHAPTER 13

Face to Face with the Stranger

"You're right, Benny," Jessie said in a shaky voice, pointing to a lean man at the counter.

Henry glanced at the tall man hunched over the counter and shrugged. "What's wrong, Jessie?"

"H-He's humming."

"So?" Henry said.

"He's humming that awful tune that I heard the night I went to the pump," she said softly.

"You can't accuse a man for humming.

107

You have to be sure, Jessie." Henry studied the unshaven man thoughtfully.

Fortunately the man didn't notice them. He was too busy reading the menu.

Violet, too, examined the man from head to foot. "I don't know," she said, remembering her encounter with the figure that had dived into the shrubbery. "I thought he was shorter."

"It's hard to tell," Henry answered, "when he's sitting down."

The lean man stirred his coffee, still humming the eerie tune. He didn't seem to care who was around him.

Jessie's eyes grew big, horrified at being so close to the stranger. "I-I'm sure!" she stammered. "I'll never forget that funny off-key melody! It's too weird. He's the one."

Henry gave her a sharp look. "Are you positive?"

Jessie stared at the man, nodding slowly. "I'm positive!"

"Then, we'd better phone the sheriff," he said quietly. He hurried to the table where Pete was sitting with his grandfather.

"Grandfather," Henry said, keeping an eye on the lean man drinking coffee. "Jessie says that's the man she heard at the pump. Should you call the sheriff?" Again Henry glanced at the stranger.

"Your grandfather told me all about the prowler and his humming," Pete said. "No need to call the sheriff, though." He chuckled. "Bill Connors comes in here at ten-thirty every day for coffee." He tilted his head in the direction of the sheriff. "That's Bill at the table next to the window."

Henry turned to his grandfather. "We're certain that man at the counter is the intruder," he said in a low voice.

"You are?" Grandfather asked, talking in a low voice. "You mustn't make a mistake."

"I'm sure," Henry said urgently.

"How do you know?" Grandfather questioned.

"That man is humming the same tune that Jessie heard at Pete's house." Henry's tone was urgent.

"Henry, you could be a detective," Grandfather said proudly.

Henry said, shaking his head, "It was Benny who spotted him."

"Jessie, go talk to the sheriff," Grandfather said, turning to find Jessie.

But Jessie had already hurried to the sheriff's side and sat across from him. "Sir," she began, "I'm Jessie Alden and we . . ."

The pleasant, round-faced man half turned to face Jessie. "Pete told me all about you kids. You're staying at his house, aren't you?" The smiling man took another bite of his doughnut.

Jessie hurriedly told him about the humming prowler.

"Don't worry," he said easily, "we'll catch the man who bothered you!"

"He's sitting at the end of the counter," Jessie said quickly.

Sheriff Connors gave the stranger a sideways glance. "Why, that's Jake Morris. He lives in town and everyone knows him. Jake's a harmless fellow. You must be mistaken. What makes you think he's the one?" He gave Jessie a doubtful look.

"I heard him humming the tune that he

was humming when I went to the pump one night. He was watching our house!" Jessie bit her underlip, afraid the man would get away. Why didn't the sheriff do something! Her heart began to pound.

"Now, I can't arrest everyone who hums a certain tune," the sheriff said with a grin. "Besides, I don't hear him humming."

Jessie glanced at the stranger. Sure enough, he'd stopped. Jessie impatiently tapped her fingers on the tabletop.

When the sheriff noticed how worried she was, he continued in a soothing voice, "Don't you worry, Jessie. We'll catch the man who tried to rob you."

"He's the one. I'm positive!" Jessie exclaimed. "Please, hurry!"

The sheriff shook his head. "Relax! I'm not arresting anyone because they're humming a tune!"

In despair, Jessie twisted around. She looked at Henry and shook her head. Again she turned and studied the man at the far end of the counter. If only there were something to prove he was the intruder!

Henry was still standing beside Grand-father and Pete when all at once his eyes narrowed. There was no doubt about it — Jessie was right! That man was the guilty one! Out of the man's back pocket jutted a gray work glove. The very glove that matched the one he had found in the library! He pulled it from his pocket. "Sheriff!" Henry said grimly. "See this glove?" Triumphantly, he held it before the sheriff's eyes.

The sheriff grunted. "I see it."

"It matches the one that man has in his pocket!" Henry slapped the glove back and forth in his hands. "Sheriff, this glove was found on a shelf in the library! The prowler wore it when he handled the books in his hunt for the sword."

The sheriff's eyes widened. "Is that so?" Gently he placed his doughnut back on the plate and stood.

The thin-faced man glanced at the sheriff.

The sheriff stood up and hitched up his belt and holster. He moved toward the man. "Hello, Jake," he said in a friendly tone. "What are you . . . ?"

Jake's eyes narrowed suspiciously. He glanced over his shoulder and saw Jessie, Violet, Henry, and Benny. Immediately he jumped up and dashed into the men's room.

Henry whirled about, and along with the sheriff he rushed at the door, but when Sheriff Connors tried the knob, it was locked!

Benny cried, "He's gone!"

"Not by a long shot," the sheriff yelled. Putting his shoulder to the door, he heaved against it with all his might. The door splintered, but remained shut.

Henry shouted, "He'll go out the back!"

"There's only a high window," Pete said reassuringly.

The sheriff looked at Pete, and Pete looked at the sheriff.

The plump sheriff raced to the front door, but in a flash, Henry was outside ahead of him. Henry's thoughts raced along with his legs. If the stranger got to his car, he'd escape for sure.

When Henry reached the back of the café, sure enough, the man had crawled out the small high window and was clinging to the

windowsill, his long legs dangling in midair. He was about to drop to the ground and escape! Henry realized he had to stop him any way that he could! He dived for the man's legs, wrapping his arms about his ankles and holding on tight! "I've got him!" he yelled.

Huffing and puffing, the sheriff finally appeared around the corner. "Let him go, lad," he commanded.

By this time Benny and the others had arrived. "You caught the mean man!" Benny shouted. "Good, Henry!"

Henry let go of the man's legs, and Jake released his hold on the sill, dropping to the ground. He glared at Henry. "You!" he snarled. His eyes glittered as he glanced at each Alden. "You all meddled in things that don't concern you!"

Jessie shuddered, glancing at the man's bony long fingers. "I'm glad you caught him," she murmured.

"You bet I have," the sheriff said grimly. "Jake, I can't believe this. But it must be true. Mike Johnson mentioned someone humming before he switched on the light in his jewelry store the night he was robbed."

Jake glared at the sheriff and shifted uneasily.

Sheriff Connors nodded knowingly. "We'll find out, Jake, if you're the one who's been stealing things around here. A valuable musket and an old dagger from Lamont's Antique Store were stolen, too." He took a breath. "And you must have been the one who robbed Mrs. Tate of her diamond ring!" He scratched his head. "And, by golly, you must have stolen the antique maps from Tom Davis's map and coin shop. And the set of gold coins he had! Why, if you're the one, and I think you are, every store owner will be tickled pink that you're behind bars."

"Hah!" the thin-faced man had a guilty look in his close-set eyes. He knew he'd been found out. "If it hadn't been for these four kids," he snarled, "I could have gotten my hands on a Civil War sword!"

"How did you know about the sword?" Jessie asked. "We didn't tell a soul."

Jake laughed. "You told one person." He motioned toward Henry. "He told your grandfather on the phone. I was in a booth here and I overheard him."

"I never even noticed you," Henry said.

"Move, Jake!" Sheriff Connors ordered, giving him a shove. "We're taking a ride to the county station. Won't the boys be surprised to see you?"

With his hands in the air, Jake walked to the squad car, the sheriff in back of him. Before he got in, he gave the Aldens a dark scowl.

"Whew," Benny said, mopping his forehead. "I'm glad we caught him. He could have stolen our sword and kept it for himself!"

"You're right, Benny." Violet laughed, throwing an arm about Benny's shoulder. "That sword belongs in a museum. For everyone!"

"The milk and cookies are on me!" Pete said in a loud voice.

Happily everyone followed Pete back into the café. The stranger was going to jail, and they were safe at last!

Benny's round face lit up when he saw the

big chocolate cookies and the cold, frothy milk. "My heart was beating fast when we caught that mean man! It made me hungry!"

Everyone laughed and finished the treat.

Miguel and his father soon stood up to leave.

"Thank you for everything," Pedro Morales said warmly.

"Yes," echoed Miguel. "Thank you." His dark eyes sparkled as he smiled at everyone.

"Mr. Morales," Grandfather asked, "what will you do without a fishing boat?"

Pedro shrugged. "I have my son. I don't need anything else!"

"We'll all stay one more day," Grandfather Alden said firmly. "Tomorrow I want you to meet me at the boatyard at two o'clock. You are to pick out the best fishing boat afloat!"

Pedro smiled, which lit up his weather-beaten face. "How can I repay you?"

"Bring us some fish once in awhile," Grandfather answered with a smile.

"Yes," Benny said loudly. "And lobsters, too."

"Every week!" Pedro promised. He left with his arm around Miguel.

The next morning Grandfather and his grandchildren drove to the boatyard. Pedro and Miguel were standing by a large boat, waiting for them.

"Hi!" Benny yelled, racing toward Miguel. "I'll help you choose a boat!"

Miguel grinned. He was lucky to have such wonderful friends.

Row after row of boats surrounded them. Big boats, small boats, fishing boats, speed boats, row boats, and sailboats.

Grandfather, his arms folded, leaned against a blue and white yacht. His eyes twinkled. "Have you picked out a boat, Mr. Morales?" he asked.

Pedro smiled shyly. "No, Mr. Alden," he responded. "That's up to you."

Benny dashed toward a large gray boat with clean long lines. "This one!" he shouted.

Grandfather raised an eyebrow. "What do you think, Mr. Morales?"

Pedro ran his fingers over the smooth surface. "It's a beauty. Benny has chosen the best boat on the lot."

"Then it's settled," Grandfather said, placing a hand on Pedro's shoulder. He motioned to the salesman and completed the sale.

With tears in his eyes, Pedro heartily shook Grandfather's hand. "I'll never forget you."

Jessie and Violet hugged Miguel, and the slender boy gazed at them for a moment, then turned away with his father.

Pedro and Miguel stopped once at the entrance and waved, and then they were gone.

"I'll miss Miguel," Benny said sadly.

"We all will," Violet said softly.

Without a word they joined Grandfather and went home.

The next week, Grandfather Alden convinced the City Council that the library should be saved and, because of its age and the hidden sword, be given landmark status.

Several months later, he took his grandchildren on a trip to Boston to visit the Boston Museum. Displayed in a beautiful glass case was their Civil War sword. It no longer was in rusty pieces but in one long blade.

The blade shimmered. Nearby was the letter from General Meade.

"We found the sword," Violet said proudly.

"Yes," Jessie said. "We found an American treasure. That's one of the best things we've ever done!"

"No," Benny piped up. "The best thing was helping Miguel and his father."

They laughed, knowing that Benny was right!

And they left the museum feeling warm and good. Not, however, because they'd saved a library and discovered a Civil War sword, but because they'd helped someone as nice as Miguel and his father.

GERTRUDE CHANDLER WARNER discovered when she was teaching that many readers who like an exciting story could find no books that were both easy and fun to read. She decided to try to meet this need, and her first book, *The Boxcar Children*, quickly proved she had succeeded.

Miss Warner drew on her own experiences to write the mystery. As a child she spent hours watching trains go by on the tracks opposite her family home. She often dreamed about what it would be like to set up housekeeping in a caboose or freight car — the situation the Alden children find themselves in.

When Miss Warner received requests for more adventures involving Henry, Jessie, Violet, and Benny Alden, she began additional stories. In each, she chose a special setting and introduced unusual or eccentric characters who liked the unpredictable.

While the mystery element is central to each of Miss Warner's books, she never thought of them as strictly juvenile mysteries. She liked to stress the Aldens' independence and resourcefulness and their solid New England devotion to using up and making do. The Aldens go about most of their adventures with as little adult supervision as possible — something else that delights young readers.

Miss Warner lived in Putnam, Connecticut, until her death in 1979. During her lifetime, she received hundreds of letters from girls and boys telling her how much they liked her books.